# GOOD GIRL
# GONE WIFE

## LISA DUBLIN

LISA M DUBLIN

# Kindle a burning

◆ ◆ ◆

**"Kindle A Burning" is a series of fictional books that explores marriage in all its ups and downs, comedy, tragedy and yes, magic. 'Good Girl Gone Wife' is the first in this series.**

# DEDICATION

**This book is for my aunts, Lynn, Jean, Marie and Brenda.**
**I'm forever branded with your love.**

## In Thanks

**To God:** Hey God, El Elyon, thanks for imparting wisdom to this daughter of yours. You are my Daddy and I am your favored daughter.

**To my husband:** Thanks Hil; every day, you settle my heart and our home. And I still have a crush on you, smh.

**To my mentor:** Mac D (MacDonald Dixon), thank you so very much. You came through with the vengeance of a literary godfather to help me get this book published. You rock.

# PART 1: THE FIGHT

When you start to scratch a cheating husband's car, you feel so good. You feel like you're raking his deceitfully handsome face. Crexxx. Take your time, do it in a straight line. Don't go and just scratch it all over because that will draw attention to you in a deserted parking lot at the biggest mall in Edmonton, in the middle of the night. So, move in a straight line. Start at the headlight, key the hood, scrape all the way to the driver's door. He hurt you again, he will pay for that. He is with her, not with you, and on top of that, she is white. What is he thinking?

Kayla kept close to the body of the silver Honda Civic, pretending to be fumbling with something, in case the cameras caught her in the act. She looked around. Yes, there were cameras in the parking lot of WEM, but Simon would never dare report her, would he? And if a security guard came up, she could always argue that it was her car too. After all, she was married to the low life.

In the middle of her sabotage however, her heart broke. What was the point? Damaging his car would not make Simon come back to her. She still felt like breaking the windshield and slashing the tires, anything to hurt Simon. He needed to feel exactly what she was going through right now. But it was pitifully clear to her that these actions were only momentarily satisfying, an act of helplessness. She turned around in tears and headed for her own car, the bright Fantasyland logo was electric white and mocking against the clear October sky. Somewhere, in that hotel, Simon was holed up with a woman—she knew that for sure; she had the texts to prove it. She had been tracking his phone for the last three weeks, and wished she could un-see what she had seen. The man was a cheat, a whore; he was pimping himself to his manager.

The sobs hiccupped, deep, out from her chest—her breasts heaved— as she backed out of the parking lot and sped down 170 Street. Her so-called revenge felt anything but. There was no vindication, there was no triumph in what she had just done. In fact, there was this terrible truth seeping through the shreds of her heart, that if she had really been in control of the situation, if she had believed that she could get Simon to stop cheating on her, she would never have keyed his car. It looked desperate because it was.

And why did she feel helpless? She could not stop the lies from coming out, because she knew him. Nothing she said could make him stop doing what he wanted to do. It had always been that way. The first time Simon cheated on her, with that Anna girl from his office, it had been the same thing. He became distant, but seemingly more caring. He became furtive and secretive, reading text messages in the bathroom under the pretext of using the toilet. He would go out at night when he thought she was asleep and be as bright and cheery next morning. She had acted like a bitch and smashed his Blackberry, threatening to come to his workplace and make a scene. He just apologized and continued right along in the same vein as if he could do the two things together, love her and cheat on her like they were both natural phenomena. Then one day it just stopped. Kayla felt vindicated, her man had come back to her— she had fought and won. Things went back to normal in their household, they even resumed talking about having children, until about six months later when a mutual friend gave her the whole story. The Anna chick migrated to New York because Simon would not leave his marriage for her. Simon came back because he didn't have another option. It had nothing to do with choosing his wife. Nothing to do with her attempts to get him to leave his side chick.

Kayla did not sleep that night. Although it was cold, already in low single digits, a little below normal for a Fall night in October, she opened the blinds so she could stare out of their apartment at all the static lights, all over the condo complex. That was one thing about Edmonton. Living in the suburbs you realized that the lights did not wink. They were just static, steady lights, as boring as they come. She put her socked feet up on the center table, a cup of Bwaden tea in her hand, and waited for her husband to come home. How had she ended up here? She had done everything she was supposed to do, she had been faithful, took good care of him, well, except for cooking, which she didn't particularly care for. She had always been a good woman to him, but here she was again, alone, waiting for him to come home.

Simon walked into the condo at 2:02 am, took one look at her bundled up on the sofa, feet curled under her, and said: "Oh, you're up, Kay?"

"Where were you?"

"I told you I was staying late at work. And then some crazy person vandalized my car, so I went looking around the parking lot to see if anyone saw anything."

"Did they?"

"Did they what?"

"Did anyone see anything?"

"No, the security guards were making the rounds, so they were in another part of the building. I'll check the cameras tomorrow."

"So where were you working?"

"What do you mean, where was I working?" Simon was very convincing, incredulous almost, making Kayla feel stupid for asking him questions.

"What do I mean? Where were you working? What do I MEAN?" *implied yelling*

Kayla sprung up like a wild animal suddenly free of its cage. "You did not happen to be parked in the parking lot of FantasyLand Hotel at WEM, would you? That was not you, Simon? Tell me that was not you."

"I don't know what you're talking about, Kayla. I was at work." Simon removed his corduroy jacket slowly, hung it in the closet, keeping his back turned to Kayla. She creeped up behind him.

"Yeah, that must have been a lot of work screwing her. What did she offer you? A promotion? So you're a prostitute now? Or maybe you're just trying to hurt me?"

He didn't say anything. Kayla could see he was stalling for time. He had already hung up his jacket and was fumbling with the buttons, as if he ever buttoned his jacket when he hung it in the coat rack.

"Simon, answer me! Where were you? Who were you with?" No answer.

He kept on fumbling with the stupid jacket.

"Simon, were you or were you not with another woman at Fantasyland Hotel?" He just shook his head and refused to look up or look around.

Kayla snapped. She came at him with her fists, crying,

flailing and very angry; she shoved him against the door. "I've been good to you, why are you doing this to me again? Why?" She pummeled his back.

Simon whipped around and grabbed her hands. It was then she saw the calm in his eyes, calm, in the face of her anger. In that instant she knew she would not win. He had made up his mind to do what he wanted, whenever he wanted. She knew it and felt it. The helplessness made her want to fight him for making her feel so useless, at the mercy of his love. His strong arms held her fists away from his face. Kayla tried to kick him; he blocked her leg with his knee, and a shooting pain raced through her shin. She screamed and sank to the floor; he let go of her arms and she fell grabbing at his legs, but he shook her off.

"Kayla, Kayla, stop it!"

"You stop! How could you do this to me again Simon? I am your wife. You're with that woman. I know because I followed you. I saw your car. I'm the one that scratched it up."

*Battered Women's Syndrome*

She grabbed his leg and without thinking sank her teeth into his ankle, the only part of him she had access to now.

Simon howled.

"Bitch!" he said and shoved her further away from him. Kayla's back hit the island and her scream split the air; it cut through the violence, and they snapped out of it. Simon ran over to Kayla and helped her up into his arms. She was crying, her back hurt, her arms throbbed where he had grabbed her, but her heart hurt the most, he had deceived her.

*relateable ?*

So why was it she was letting him undress her? What trash of a woman was she to want to lay down with Simon after he had just cheated on her. He held her close, kissed her tears, reached for the thick blanket they kept hidden behind the sofa, the navy-blue velveteen, the one they bought at Costco last Christmas. Simon tried to hush her tears away, hastily tucking the blanket around them like old times. He was sorry, she could tell, but it was not enough to quiet their bodies, volatile and bewildered at the advent of this new violence. Kayla felt nothing as he thumped his rhythm against her body, rigid, struggling to capture her soul again. A couple hours later, his watch began to vibrate on his wrist and it woke them up. Kayla kept her eyes closed as he swung his arm up from around her, uncoupled his body from hers and sprung to his feet. She kept her eyes closed as he fixed the blanket around her, making sure she was warm. She didn't turn, didn't acknowledge him, didn't say anything. She knew that he knew that she was awake. She had caught her breath and slowed her breathing, something they both did when they were awake but didn't want to talk.

Kayla could hardly wait for Simon to leave. She was angry, humiliated and feeling very disgusted with herself. She curled up under the heavy blanket, hurting and sore all over, and grateful for the darkness. Simon must have drawn the curtains while she was asleep. The only sliver of daylight was carelessly peeping through the space where the blinds met or didn't quite meet.

She heard him put on the coffee maker, then he went to the shower; still she did not budge. Kayla wanted so much to get up and go to her bed, but if it meant she had to look in her cheating husband's face, or speak to him, she would stay right there, she did not have words for him. When Simon closed the door some thirty minutes later, Kayla flung the covers back, picked up her clothes from the floor and headed for the bathroom.

# PART 2: OLIVE CENTRICK

About 10:30 that morning, someone rapped on the front door. Kayla was sitting in the living room, busy working on a client's Questrade account. She looked up at the door in surprise, as if expecting to see who was on the other side. The person knocked again, Kayla walked to the peephole and looked.  It was the lady next door she had never spoken to, the nosey looking one.

"Hi, good morning," the lady said when Kayla opened the door.

"Good morning, hi," Kayla responded, squirming a little under the lady's piercing gaze. People complained about that woman, she was always reporting transgressions to the Condo board, so what now?

"Are you okay? I heard some commotion last night."

Kayla was taken aback but relaxed quickly; the lady had a Caribbean accent, no wonder she was extra nosey.

"Oh, it's okay. We're fine. We had an argument, that's all, sorry for the disturbance."

The lady said nothing, just continued to stare at Kayla.

"Can I help you with anything else?" Kayla blurted, uncomfortably irritated at her lies.

"Yes, I wonder if you can help me get something in my home. I had a hip replacement, and it is still bothering me, but I want to bring down the winter blankets from my closet. They are all the way at the top. That cold weather is coming fast."

"Yeah, okay, I'll come by in a while?"

"Okay, thank you." She ambled off, not looking as if she had a hip replacement at all.

Kayla put on a light jacket over her sweats, slipped on her Crocs and headed over to the unit next to hers. The old lady opened the door before she could complete her knock. "Come in, I'm Olive Centrick by the way; I don't think we ever spoke?"

Kayla stuck out her hand and their palms embraced. Olive's hand was warm and dry. No extra stuff. Kayla slipped out of her Crocs and followed the lady up the stairs, gazing around curiously as one did in other peoples' homes for the first time. The house smelled of warm apples, maybe Olive was making apple pie? The walls were a warm, clean white, the baseboards were clean too and pristine, and every piece of furniture was in place. Kayla wished she could keep a clean house like that. Cleaning got her very tired and, frankly, she thought she could be using her time more effectively, making money online as an investment broker. The only thing was that she hated a dirty house, and so did Simon. So a couple times a week, she would do spot cleaning. Don't ask her about under the beds or behind the tv area. 'Don't see, don't clean' was her motto. In any case, they hired a cleaning lady, an immigrant from Tanzania, to do the deep cleaning once a month.

She snapped out of her silent narrative as Olive got to the top of the stairs and pulled open the door of the linen closet.

"The blankets are up there", she said, wincing and rubbing her hip. "My son's friend comes to help me pack them away every April or so, when he comes to do some gardening for me. My son is in the Netherlands. Ten years now. He's married to a white girl. Gave me two grandchildren. So he is busy with his own life over there. I usually get a neighbor to help me bring the blankets down in the Fall."

Kayla nodded.

"The step ladder is in my room, behind you. If you grab it you should be able to reach up and bring down the blanket. I think you'll be able to reach them, no? You are way taller than me". She sized Kayla up and down. "How tall are you?"

"I'm 5 ft 6". You?

"Yeah, I'm 5 ft 4", Olive replied as she motioned to Kayla to take the step ladder behind her, in her bedroom.

Kayla entered a peaceful room. She was not sure what made it so serene - if it was the fresh flowers on the dresser, a bloom of hydrangeas, pink, purple and blue, or the calming mint green of the walls, or the big, wooden, oval-framed picture of Olive and her husband on their wedding day. They were both laughing - him grinning at her, and Olive with her neck flung back, veil billowing in the back of her, seeming to laugh from her belly as she gazed at the camera, her slender hands resting firmly on her new husband's lapels. The bed was elaborate. It was a queen-sized bed with all the fancy pillows, pillowcases and cushions gathered like a clustered community, the way they were arranged. But what was that on the nightstand next to Olive's side of the bed. Zig Zags? And a baggie of weed? To be honest, there was a faint smell of something inside the room.

She grabbed the step ladder, which was by the door, and went back into the hallway.

She winced as she climbed and pulled the thick

bedspread from the top of the closet. Her back hurt her where Simon had thrown her against the cupboard last night. She stiffened a little.

"What's wrong?" Olive asked quickly.

It must have been because Kayla hesitated for one half of a second before responding, that Olive asked the next question.

"Did he hit you last night?"

Why was she responding? Kayla did not even feign ignorance or surprise.

"No he didn't. I gave as good as I got." She handed the first comforter to Olive. "We don't ever fight like that honestly, but he is cheating again and I'm not standing for it. It's his boss. Some white chick downtown called Emily."

She yanked the last big comforter from the closet with such force that she almost toppled off the step ladder.

"Steady, steady," Olive's voice was calm and quiet. She put her hand out to hold Kayla, and Kayla stiffened again.

"Okay, come downstairs. I'll rub your back with some ointment I have there."

There was no room to say no to Olive's command. There was no even trying to say no. This woman was feeling very safe.

After Olive had tucked away the two comforters in the bottom of her closet, and after she had made Kayla some good old bwaden tea, she brought out a vial of Vicks Vaporub. When she opened it though, Kayla saw the dark ointment and smelled the slightly ripe smell of Friar's Balsam, a smell she was only too familiar with. Back home in Saint Lucia, people used that ointment to heal swellings and sore areas where you got hit or knocked hard. The smell reminded her of home.

"I know that smell. That's a fixion. Y'all use that here in

Canada, Miss Olive?" Kayla asked, curious.

"That's a Grenadian remedy too. I forgot what they call it back home, but Canadians would never use that here. It's too primitive for them," Olive chuckled. "But it works."

"So you're from Grenada?"

"Yes, but I came to Mississauga in 1970 and then we moved to Edmonton in 1983, just in time for the Ralph cuts. I've lived most of my life here."

Olive scooped some of the ointment into her hands and motioned to Kayla to turn around with her back to her.

"Raise your top. I'll rub it for you." Kayla lifted her sweater so Olive could rub her lower back with the mixture. Olive unclasped her bra and got to work. Kayla marveled that she was not in the least bit embarrassed to find herself in a stranger's kitchen, boobs a bit exposed, getting 'rubbed'. It all had to do with the old lady's spirit. She just seemed so...whole, so peaceful, in spite of being nosey.

"Where does it hurt?" Olive asked. Kayla, hands at her sides holding up her sweater, twisted to the right and nodded downwards. "My lower back, on the right. I don't think Simon meant to do it, but I was biting his ankle and he tried to push me away; that's what happened."

"So you were fighting like a dog then, biting?" Olive alleged, and then she laughed. Kayla was upset a little, but the old lady's levity was contagious, and she sniffed as she remembered the way she grabbed Simon's ankle and sank her teeth into his ankle.

'Yeah, I was not thinking; it's not funny. I honestly don't know what to do. He's cheating again and nothing I do stops him."

"What have you tried?"

Kayla could feel the frustration; hot tears came to her eyes. She shrugged as Olive smeared the ointment on her sore lower back. It was a wee bit cold.

"What do you mean what I have tried? I found out about him and Emily a month ago, and I've been tracking his phone. I only confronted him last night because he slept at a hotel with her."

"What did he say?"

"Nothing. He never admits. That's the second time. The first time was in Saint Lucia, where I'm from."

"Oh, that's your accent— been trying to trace it ever since I first spoke to you."

"Yeah, we're both from Saint Lucia."

Olive's hands grasped and released, kneaded, and squeezed both sides of Kayla's back. It hurt so much when she worked her way into the muscle that Kayla gave little pfft puff sounds, between breaths.

"Your husband ever cheated on you?" Kayla asked, her voice ragged with hurt.

Olive took her time to release the pain inside her with every knead and squeeze. "Yes, he did it a few times, until I learned to fight like a wife."

Kayla heard the words like a dog whistle. "What do you mean, fight like a wife?"

"Well, it is either you fight like the man is not yours - you bite him, punch him, insult him, and pretend you hate him, or you take your stand as the wife and fight like you win already. Before God he is yours, so you start with God."

That only frustrated Kayla, and she squirmed under Olive's massaging touch.

"I don't think that applies to me. You fight like a wife when you have a husband that will listen. The first time Simon cheated on me, nothing could make him leave that girl. The affair ended only because she moved to New York. I'm not enough for him, although I love him, and I thought he loved me back."

"Oh no! You're fighting from the angle that you're not enough for him. Of course, you will end up biting his ankles and doing crazy things like that. You young girl, you don't know men. That man loves you. I saw y'all the other day when he brought the new car home. I could see it all over his face, he was happy to buy it for you."

"Oh ho, so the neighbors are right when they call you nosey?" Kayla teased, mimicking the old lady's accent. "I heard that about you when we first moved in." She smiled an impish smile, teasing Olive so she would not have to think about the hard questions she was being forced to ask herself. Olive seemed unaffected.

"Well if I don't watch, they will get away with murder in this condo village. I had to call the property manager the other day because someone was parked in my parking stall. How is that fair? I pay just like everyone else, so I expect things to be done a certain way."

"Yeah, I had to reach out to the condo board a couple of times too! My car got stuck in the snow because they did not clear the parking lot for a whole three days after that last snowstorm."

"So you see my point? We pay our condo fees, therefore we have a right to demand certain services, not so? It's the same thing with marriage. What should you reasonably expect from your guy?"

"I expected him to love me and…and make me feel safe," Kayla blurted out,

"But I guess it won't ever happen. When he does not come home on time or I don't hear from him for a couple hours, my heart beats so fast that I can't do anything but worry that he might be cheating on me. I didn't sign up for this kind of relationship."

"So what do you do?" Olive patted Kayla's back clasped her bra back, and gently pulled down her sweatshirt. "There, I'm finished now. No more useless fighting with your husband. You must learn to win." She walked to the kitchen and turned on the stove under the saucepan with the bois d'inde tea.

"Let me get you some more tea. You want some more?"

Kayla nodded because that had not been a question at all.

"I don't know what to do. We don't have any family here, nobody to talk to him and Simon won't listen to me. So ever since I found out, I push him away, no sex. If he's getting from outside good for him."

Why was Miss Olive looking at her with such strange eyes, as if she knew only last night she slept with Simon?

"Okay, I guess you'll continue to do your thing and please yourself." Olive looked through Kayla, and Kayla blushed. That was not just a clap-back. How did she know …? Like how could she know? She hurried over the question by gulping down almost all the herbal tea. Olive just continued to gaze at her. She was chuckling, enjoying Kayla's discomfort.

"Before God he is yours, that's where you start. God will deal with men who have been treacherous in their marriage. That's what the Good Book says."

"Oh well," Kayla was non-committal. She used to be in God, church, and all, but tempered her close relationship with the Big Man since that first instance of adultery back home. Frankly, she felt betrayed by both God and Simon, so she had settled for just being good. It was easy. She saw her mother do it for years. Her mother had been a good wife to her father - a Pastor, no less - and then after her father's first affair, she became indifferent at home. She no longer sang, no longer smiled, just kept her head down and died a little every day, while her father became false and more pompous by the hour. It was not long before her body surrendered to breast cancer. Kayla's mom was fifty-eight. A year later, her father was expelled from his own church when the side chick confessed to the affair in a testimony before the entire congregation.

Kayla thought life for her would be different, after all, Simon was not a Pastor and showed none of her father's roving eye characteristics, although had she listened to everyday gossip she would have heard: girls tend to marry men like their fathers. After Simon cheated the first time, Kayla understood how her mother coped; it was easier that way. If you kept your head down, and didn't bother God, he wouldn't bother you. Be a dutiful wife and get God and the world to leave you alone. Like everyone else, she resigned herself to just being a good wife. She didn't drink, she didn't smoke, and didn't cheat on her man. She just wanted God and the whole set of men (with problematic zips) to leave her alone.

"Oh well what? You look like you knew God and now you don't care for him."

Kayla was really feeling exposed now, definitely naked.

"God didn't step in the first time. The woman had to migrate overseas for me to get my man back. I'm ashamed of that. Where's God in all that."

"There was God in your marriage from the time you and him joined together. A marriage is spiritual. It's not just a piece of paper you signed. So that's where you start the fight. Stop biting and cussing him, and fight with your legal paper."

"My legal paper? No lawyers please."

Miss Olive seemed suddenly far away. "There are some

things only God can break, and other things only he can put together."

"Miss Olive, you're sounding very strange right now."

She snapped back from her reverie, causing Kayla to wonder if the older woman was a bit senile.

"Come back here tomorrow. Spend a little time with me. I don't like to see young people fighting like how y'all were last night. And you must be careful coz one of these real nosey white people here will be quick to call police on Simon."

"Okay, I'll come tomorrow." It's not like she had a whole lot doing anyways. She had to update a couple clients' accounts, but tomorrow was supposed to be her no-meeting day. She got up to leave, and Olive walked her to the door.

"And don't be fighting tonight. If you knew he was yours— what you say his name was again? Simon?" Kayla nodded. "Okay, so if you knew for sure that Simon was your husband and that you would get him back and this woman would not be a threat, what would you do tonight when he got home?"

Kayla paused for a while. Yeah, what would she do? Why did that question relax her a bit? Why did she feel a little more empowered? Simon was not just her lawfully wedded husband, she was also spiritually bonded to him too. Why did that question make her look for an answer from a position of settled confidence?

"I will not bite him again for sure," both she and Olive laughed at how ridiculous she sounded. "I would not quarrel. I would not say anything. I would wait until we were both calm and settled and ask him what's going on."

"Well, do that. And if you really want to get him nervous, cook for him; he won't know what you're thinking. It's a game for him, so you have to change the mode of play."

Kayla's mind went back to the portrait hanging in Olive's bedroom.

"How long were you married, Miss Olive?" Kayla asked.

"Thirty-one years," Olive replied. "And I don't regret being married to Mr. Handsome. He could still light my fire right up until he died," her whole face lit up as she spoke about Oscar.

"How long ago?"

"Eleven years next month. But run along, you have work to do. And come for about 10 tomorrow. I'll talk to you then."

_Well said_

# PART 3: CHANGE THE PLAY

Dinner was baked asparagus, basmati rice and seared salmon in lemon butter. She didn't dish it out, just left it all there in the pot; the few times she cooked, she never dished out his food, he did not deserve that kind of treatment.

To her surprise, Simon walked through the door earlier than usual. He was still feeling guilty about hurting her the night before. Through the open blinds, she saw when he pulled up into the parking lot. By the time he got his key through the door, Kayla was seated at the kitchen table, pretending she was speaking virtually with a client, she wanted to observe his reaction when he walked in and smelled cooked food. He looked over at her looking at him, he nodded, she caught his look of surprise, before that emotion got smothered on an unexpressive, sullen face. She nodded back, pretending she was on a call all the while. He stayed in the coat rack area for a couple minutes; she could tell he was confused, perhaps expecting hostility, or even violence, like in the past. She continued with her imaginary online client through her head mic.. She kept on "uhmming" and "uh huhhing" into the phone, Simon passed around her and headed straight for the stove. Shucks. She swiped her screen and landed on a random Kajabi page. Hopefully he did not have time to notice that she had been watching Afropop videos on Youtube. He looked at the tray of baked salmon, uncovered the rice cooker, and stared at the dining table set for two. He rubbed hard on the scalp at the back of his head. Yep. Olive was right. He did not expect this. Now, what should she do? Kayla was not quite sure.

She said her 'goodbyes' on the phone, clicked the MacBook and removed her headset. Silence. He took the plates and started dishing out the food. "Thanks," he muttered. "The food looks good."

Kayla felt a rage bubbling within her. Why was she angry? Olive had not prepared her for that. The gall of the man to think that he could throw her across the floor one night and then come home to salmon and asparagus the next. For some reason, she thought of Olive's firm hands kneading her back, and she calmed down. Steady, Kayla. Steady. They sat down in silence at the dining table.

"Thanks," he said again, and looked at her with those knowing eyes of his as he handed her the plate modestly piled. Was he flirting right now? Men's moods could be confusing, she stared back at him, and he observed.

"We need to talk, Simon."

He sighed but didn't say a thing.

Kayla shoveled a fork-full of rice into her mouth. This new style confrontation was taking all the self-control she possessed.

Simon ate everything on his plate, burped, got up and went to the stove for a second helping of salmon, came back and sat down.

"We need to talk."

"Okay, can we talk after we eat?" He seemed annoyed; his old, arrogant self was coming out.

Kayla snapped. She pushed the plate away from her, knocking Simon's plate against his wine glass and spilled a little on the tablecloth. She got up and slammed her chair into the table.

"Okay, let's talk when you're good and ready about your adultery. I'm ready when you are." *Knead, Olive, knead; mentally she batted the old woman's hands away. This was not working. To hell with Olive tun.*

The entire atmosphere changed immediately; Kayla didn't need to look at Simon to understand his confusion. She gathered her laptop and notebook from the kitchen table, so much for fighting like a wife—whatever that means. So much for trying to talk. You cannot talk to a cheating man. You cannot reason with a low life. She should never have followed Simon to Canada. She should have stayed in Saint Lucia and made her life there by herself. She should have left him the first time he cheated. *Yeah, but you love him*, a stupid, cheeky voice reminded her, inserting itself into the hurricane of her thoughts. *Yeah, but you love him, you love him, you love him. You just want him to want you and you alone. You know that. You know that. You know that. And you don't know what to do.* She started crying and couldn't stop. It would be the spare room for her again tonight.

The bed was cold and uncomfortable, but she slid in and tucked the thick, plush comforter around her. She popped in her headphones and put on the Sleep Country app. It was the only way she could fall asleep with all that was running around in her head. She did not hear when Simon tried the door but found it locked; she did not hear when he softly called her name. She did not feel his presence outside for a full five minutes, just waiting. All she heard was the storm in her head, raging.

# PART 4: HOW COULD HE BE A KING?

Olive was watching the Jeffersons on CTV. Kayla plopped down on one of the white leather chairs. Why did she feel so at home here? She looked around, again marveling at how everything was in place, every picture on the mantle reflected pure, clean glass; every plant in the corner glistened, every baseboard was clean, the runner in the hallway undisturbed. Kayla wished her home could look like that; well minus the faint smell of weed, that always hung in the air.

"You look like you had a rough night. Everything okay?" Olive asked, her eyes riveted to the tv screen.

"Well, I think I blew it with Simon again. I cooked, like you said. But when I saw him eating so heartily, I just flipped and quarreled with him. I let him have it and slept in the spare room."

"Of course, you would be upset, if you cooked out of the goodness of your heart and then realized he actually was hungry." Olive chuckled and Kayla felt stupid.

She sighed, hoping Olive would stop watching TV and talk to her. Her sighs and restless movements did not work, and they watched an entire episode of The Jeffersons before

Olive asked her to get her a cup of tea from the kitchen. Today it was ginger root tea. Kayla heated the saucepan and put some honey instead of sugar in each mug. For good measure, she added a dash of lemon as well. When Kayla returned with steaming mugs to the dining room table, Olive switched the TV off with the remote.

"So how is Simon?" Olive smiled at last.

"I don't know. I didn't see him this morning. I slept in the spare room as I told you."

"Why did you sleep in the spare room?"

"Because he does not deserve me."

"So how you plan to resolve that?"

"I don't know. He's a man. He'll do what he wants, no matter what I say."

"But you're his wife. He married you."

"Yeah, tell him that."

"That's your job to tell it to him in a thousand ways but do it so he understands."

"I've fought, I've flattered his sorry ego, I've been gentle, I've been firm, I've given him sex, I've withheld it; I've cooked for him, I've eaten in front of him and he has not cared two shits."

"That's the actions of a desperate, resentful woman, Kayla."

Kayla shrugged, sipped her ginger tea; she did feel helpless that very minute.

"I don't know what to do, Miss Olive. That's the truth. If I knew how to keep my man, I would do it."

"Do you love him?"

"Yes, I love the lowlife."

"He's not a low life. Do you love him?

"Yes, I do."

"Well, does he love you?"

"I don't know."

"What don't you know?"

"I don't know if he loves me."

"What proof do you have that you don't know if he loves you?"

"Well, if you love me you won't cheat on me. So I guess I do know."

"So you think because he cheats he doesn't love you?"

"Well what else could it be?"

"What else could it be?"

Kayla looked up at Olive to see if she was playing her.

"No, I'm not joking. I'm asking you, why else could he be cheating besides not loving you."

"Maybe he has a big ego?"

"What else?"

"Maybe because he can?"

"What else?"

"Maybe he is not satisfied with me?" She blurted this one out with a sob. "I'm not enough for him. I've never been enough for him."

"What else?" Olive would not let up; she didn't coddle Kayla either.

"Maybe he wants something from me that I cannot give him."

"Cannot or have not given him."

"I don't know."

"What is that?"

"Attention, I guess. With his arrogant self, I feel like sometimes he wants all my attention."

"And what else do you think he wants that you cannot or will not give? You know your man."

Yes, Kayla knew Simon's desires. When you live with someone, you know their impulses and you feel them wanting things from you, and Kayla was good at ignoring Simon's.

"He wants me to regard him as important, I guess. But he does not deserve that from me."

"What do you want from him?"

"I want him to want only me."

"That's possible."

Kayla calmed down a little, they sipped ginger tea for a while then Olive got up and went to the kitchen and ambled back to the living room with a book. She handed it to Kayla. "I want you to start reading this from tonight. It will help you get your man back."

The name of the book was Love and Respect. Kayla opened it. In large, sprawling letters, "to Kayla from Olive. Fight Like a Wife." The date, today. Kayla looked up at Olive, surprised. "Did you buy this today? "

"Nope. I bought some copies a long time ago, so that I will always have them for when a young wife needs it."

"I guess marriage is not at all easy," Kayla surmised, as she browsed through the table of contents. "I hope we make it."

"That depends on you."

"I don't know about that. It takes two to make a marriage work."

"You're right."

"How can both things be right?"

"It takes two to make a marriage work, but one to start the change."

"I cannot change Simon."

"No you cannot. Don't even try. Work on changing yourself in this situation."

"I'm NOT doing the most, Olive. I don't need this. I could stay by myself. I don't know if I want to do the hard work to save my marriage. I don't know if I want to humble myself to a man who cheats on me. I don't know if I want any of this. My mother did it and it killed her."

"So the dildo's enough?"

Kayla was not surprised anymore. She rocked back on her butt like a big woman and heaved forward. "Yes, it is. Thanks," Olive was just too nosey.

"You not asking me how I know?"

"They said you were nosey. I don't know how you know, but I don't care."

"The bathrooms are next to each other. When you're mad at Simon, you wait till he leaves."

Kayla sucked her teeth. The woman was mad if she thought that she, Kayla Joseph, would feel ashamed for taking care of her needs.

"I don't care. I'll do what I want. If he's cheating, I am not going to sleep with him. But I have my needs. And I see you have yours too. I saw your stash in your room."

"And? Marijuana is legal in Canada. Helps with my arthritis. What exactly does your big ol' dildo help with except to deny you your man?"

"Maybe he does not want to satisfy me anymore."

"Maybe he does not know that you need him."

"Miss Olive, sex used to be so good before all this. But I'm not going to cheapen myself to Simon for sex. I'm supposed to hold back, not give in."

"Are you dating him or doing marriage? There is no room for pride in marriage. You have him and he has you. The games are for dating, not marriage."

"So showing him I need him will make him want me?"

"That's some of it. But let me ask you a question. What do you think she has that you don't?"

"For sure I'm prettier than her. She's plump, no, sorry,

she's bouftay - I cannot believe Simon settled for her. Black men tun! They always go for the worst white ones. Never the model types. They always hit it off with the rejects."

"Okay, the girl in Saint Lucia you were talking about. She was white too?"

Kayla fidgeted. She was smarting, it wasn't white girls, clearly. The one from Saint Lucia was Black, like her. It was Simon.

"She might be - what you said? Bouftay? What's that? Y'all Saint Lucians have a second language? Big?"

Kayla nodded. She could give Olive a dozen other words to describe that Emily woman.

"So, she's big, but what is she giving him that you don't?"

"I guess it's okay for her to be treated like a doormat. She must be all over him. Let her go ahead. She can have all of him."

"Doormat? Does Simon treat you like a doormat?"

"No, because I won't let him."

"You think he would if you did?"

"Well, case in point. After we had a fight, he feels okay to come home and just eat food that I cooked. That's expecting a lot."

"You cooked the food. Would you prefer if he didn't eat it?"

Kayla had not thought this through at all, at all. What if Simon had come through that door and looked at that food, and instead of sitting down to eat, said he was not hungry and gone to the bedroom? What would she have done? Her first thought would have been that he ate elsewhere, most likely by the side chick. Then she would have taken all the food and thrown it away, telling Simon exactly what a low life he was in the process. She told this with relish to Olive who seemed exasperated, "Oh, okay. How would that have worked for you? Would it solve the problem?"

So what's the problem? Kayla didn't know, she just focused on wanting to cuss Simon off.

"But he didn't have to look so satisfied? Like, 'my wife is cooking for me now. Finally, she is shaping up.' That's how he looked, and it irritated me like never before."

"Did you just hear what you said?"

Kayla looked at Miss Olive with an open face, trying to decide how to approach the question. This woman had not asked permission to wade into her life, but that is exactly what she had done. Kayla had the power to end it right away by walking out that door …. or decide to make an uncomfortable adjustment and let herself be taught things her heart told her she wanted to learn. Kayla wanted Simon more than anything else in the world. She wanted his heart the way she had it before they got married, and before the first infidelity. She didn't want to feel that he would step out on her if someone else was powerful enough to draw him away. *Okay, let's see what Olive is made of.*

"It sounds like I want him but I'm pushing him away?"

"Yep."

Kayla flipped open the book and thumbed through the table of contents. "So is this book any good? Did you use it at all?"

"Yes."

"Did you get results?"

"Why do you think I'm recommending it? I want you to read the first chapter tonight and implement whatever comes to mind and see what happens."

"But how do I deal with Simon's adultery right now?"

"You will, if you start to apply the book."

"Miss Olive, you're asking me to go against everything I believe. I don't know if I can do that. How can Simon expect respect from me if he is cheating on me?'

'What if he was made to be respected regardless?'

"So you mean respect him in spite of his adultery?"

"Nope, not that at all. Simon is wrong to cheat on you. He is not loving you the way he is supposed to. But the respect for him as a person does not depend on him cheating or not. The two things are separate."

This all sounded like mumbo jumbo to Kayla. She raised her eyebrows and shook her head. Olive continued.

"I know that sounds strange, so let's go to the One who made marriage. Do you read the Bible?"

Kayla shrugged. "I grew up in church, so yes."

"I didn't ask you if you grew up in church. I asked you, do you read the Bible?'

"No, I've been busy; the habit kind of fell off."

Olive sighed and stopped sipping her tea, she got up from the table and went to the kitchen drawer. She came back with a small Gideon Bible, and another larger, worn out one. She also carried an equally raggedy leather notebook.

"Alright Lord, alright. I hear you. I see this is a stubborn one, who will not just do what she is told. You win. I'll teach her the things her ox brain does not want to accept."

Kayla was amused as she watched Olive talk to herself; she looked like a petulant child, pouting, huffing, and puffing as she leafed through her journal to find the page she wanted. "I'm going to teach you something that you will never forget. You know why you will never forget it? Because it will change your marriage and your sex life, and your home life and it will get rid of all side chicks eventually. They will not stick. They will not be able to stay. Do you want that or do you want to be fighting every day, biting your husband's ankles, and scratching up his car.

Because you will have to do that for the rest of your life; that's where you're heading."

The way Olive put it, made the future seem glum. "No way," she shook her head. "I want a good marriage."

"Ah! who made marriage then?"

"God, I believe that."

"What did God say about marriage?"

Kayla was at a loss for words. They had done premarital counseling for six months, but a lot of what they had discussed seemed irrelevant now. "He said love my husband. He said husbands love your wives as Christ loved the church."

"Yeah, you got part of it right. In Ephesians chapter 5, Paul spoke to husbands and to wives. Here, let's read a little bit together, okay?' Olive handed the blue hardcover Gideon bible to Kayla.

"Go to Ephesians Chapter 5. You read." She reached for her glasses, heavy black and surprisingly modern frames.

"Be ye therefore followers of God, as dear children..."

"No, no, go a little further down. All of this, up until verse 22, is Paul counseling the Ephesians on how to live in the Holy Spirit, and not according to their flesh. When you have a chance, read it over again, but for now, start at verse 22. Now keep in mind Paul had just ended the whole passage before, telling all of us to submit ourselves one to another in the fear of the God, right?

Kayla nodded, thinking back to a time when this meant something to her, many years ago, before Simon cheated that first time. Then, they would go to church together, read their Bible together, pray and hold hands. None of that anymore. She refocused on Olive's now bespectacled face as the older woman prodded her to continue reading.

"Wives, submit yourselves unto your husbands, as unto

the Lord. For the husband is the head of the wife, even as Christ is the head of the church: and he is the savior of the body. Therefore, as the church is subject unto Christ, so let the wives be to their own husbands in everything."

"I wonder what the other versions of the Bible say about this?" Kayla could not help herself; she dropped the Bible on the table in derision. These words and the meaning they conveyed were not going down well with her. She could see her mother in her eyes, dutiful but sullen, up until the day she died. Kayla would not swallow that nonsense wholesale, she resisted patriarchy in every subtle way her whole life, not now was she going to accept it.

"You're looking for a softer landing, eh? I was too, back in the day. But here's the thing to consider: do you have siblings?"

"Yes, an older brother."

"That's good. What is his name?

"Jamal."

"Is Jamal more important than you?"

Kayla scoffed. "No, he just happened to be born first. That's all it is."

"There. You got it."

"Got what?"

"It's just order, not a matter of equality with how God made us male and female."

"The man is the head by design, by order of creation. The same way you can never be Jamal, never switch places with him, because only one person can be born first, it's the same thing with men. The order already happened. We are equal - men and women are equal - but in terms of order, the man comes first. That's how God organized us on earth."

Kayla was almost sick to her stomach with rage, but it

was a rage akin to hitting a bulletproof car with a barrage of bullets. It was infuriating because you just knew you would not win because the car was bulletproof. Olive's words felt too true to argue with, so she got ready to argue as furiously as she could. She was about to unleash on Olive when the old woman just nodded and told her, "I know how you feel, let's continue reading."

"Husbands, love your wives, even as Christ loved the church and gave himself for it; that he might sanctify and cleanse it with the washing of water by the word, that he might present it to himself a glorious church not having spot, or wrinkle, or any such thing; but that it should be holy and without blemish. So ought men to love their wives as their own bodies. He that loves his wife loves himself."

Kayla felt suddenly triumphant. She would have to remind Simon about that.

"What did you just read?" Olive asked.

"That Simon is not being a husband; he is not being a man."

"What if I told you the two things are separate. He is still a man, even though he is being a disobedient husband. One is his nature, the other is his role." *good reminder*

"I can't believe you would be defending him. I have proof that he is cheating. I followed them, remember? And besides, it was not the first time."

Kayla opened and closed her mouth, searching for words to express her disgust. Miss Olive again cut through the drama. "Continue reading; you're almost to the end of the chapter."

"For no man ever yet hates his own flesh; but nourishes and cherishes it even as the Lord the church: for we are members of his body, of his flesh, and of his bones. For this cause shall a man leave his father and mother, and shall be joined unto his wife, and they two shall be one flesh. This is a great mystery: but I speak concerning Christ and the church. Nevertheless, let every one of you in particular so love his wife even as himself; and the wife see that she reverences her husband."

"So what? Do I have to bow to him?"

"In some cultures, they actually do, but I'm sure Simon does not want that."

"I don't know if I can do the respect thing when Simon is being such a lowlife."

"Oi!" Olive was authoritative and took Kayla by surprise.

"Oi! If he is a low life, you are a lowlife too for marrying him. So are you a lowlife?"

"Oh hell no."

"Well, let that be the last time you wash your husband in negative words."

"But..."

"Words have power. Use them to create a future, not to tie you to what you do not want. "

"Okay, Simon is a king," Kayla said sarcastically. Her face flaming, her ego hurt. This was impossible to accept. Impossible!

"Oh yes, you said it right. What if Simon were a king? What would that make you?"

"Queen Kayla, I suppose?" Kayla's voice dripped with sarcasm, but by the time her words reached her soul, she felt good. I'm a queen. Queen Kayla.

"So listen to this please. Is it true that whether you have a productive day or not, your body still requires food and water?"

"Yes, of course."

"Right, because your body, by its very nature, is made to need food and water, no matter what you do with that

*His nature requires respect* [handwritten annotation]

body, agreed?"

"Okay, I see where you're going with this a little?"

"Where do you think I'm going with it?"

"Well according to what you're saying, I should separate Simon the man from Simon the husband. His nature requires respect even though he is messing up his role as my husband." *important* [handwritten annotation]

"So now we come to adultery. How do you deal with it? Because it is not right."

"Well, I guess .... of course I will not accept it, but how I show him is what's important. I can still respect his manhood and correct him; he's wrong for hurting me like that."

"That way, you feed both parts," Olive said, quietly.

They were silent for a moment or two, before she continued with her probing questions. "And what about what Simon needs to do for you. What do you require?"

"I'm not the average female. I don't need a man for much, Miss Olive."

Olive didn't look up, she kept thumbing through her Bible.

"I didn't ask you that. What would you like more than anything in the world from Simon?

Kayla's breath caught in her throat. She had not DARED to ask herself that question in years. Ever since the first adultery. What she wanted from Simon would make her vulnerable. Olive kept on staring at her, Kayla crawled inside herself and closed the door. It was like she was in that little treehouse at home again - the one her neighbors built for the children to enjoy. It was in the base of a big mango tree. Mr. Vaughn, the father, was a carpenter. He had built a tidy little treehouse around the base of the Tifi mango tree with a real window and a real door, although all smaller sized. Kayla would go inside sometimes, while everyone was shouting and playing Cowboys and Indians, and sit quiet, sometimes for an hour. No one ever bothered her then. And now, as she contemplated the vulnerable position of her heart, no one would bother her in there. Not even Olive.

So, what did she want? What did she want more than anything in the world? She let herself feel. What if she didn't have to check Simon's phone ever again, or feel the dread of knowing that he would go out and do what he wanted anyway? What if there were no more silent phone calls, or tiptoes to the bathroom to respond to a text? What if he came home and was open and relaxed with her, and not guarded? Kayla admitted, in the shade of her thoughts, that the thing she wanted more than anything else in the world was for Simon to choose her above everyone else.

While Miss Olive sipped her tea and thumbed through the pages of her Bible, Kayla sat in the slap of an internal whirlwind. Her world was dividing, between before the big idea and after the big idea. Olive wanted her to believe that Simon's nature as a man was different from his role as a husband. His manhood needed one thing, respect, no matter what his circumstance. Man, and husband. Man, and husband. The two things were not the same. And by the same idea, her own womanly nature was different from her role as a wife. She knew she needed love, and respect too, she wanted to be respected and not walked over, but she also needed love, whether she slept with him or not, whether she cooked for him or not, whether she paid him attention or not. She needed a place to rest her heart and know that it was safe. Kayla cried in the coolness of her mind. Olive sipped and didn't look up. She only said, "There now", and continued to read and make some notes.

Kayla wept a good bit and then slowly wiped her eyes.

It was ringing true for her. This truth was pristine and shining, in a new place in her heart.

"So tonight," Miss Olive continued, you're going to read Chapter 1 of this book, and do one thing to test it out when Simon comes home. The book is like an antibiotic. It starts to work right away because it goes straight to the site of the disease."

Kayla was a mess; she didn't want to go home just yet.

"Can I stay here and read a little?" she asked softly.

"Yeah, you can stay for a while, but I'm going to take a nap soon, so you will have to see yourself out."

"The weed is wearing off?" Kayla chuckled. Boy, she enjoyed teasing this woman, if just to lighten her own load.

"I wonder how you know about the feeling. Hmmm?" Olive shot back, but she too was chuckling, and shaking her head. "You are brazen for a young woman, yes."

As if to signal that the lesson was done for the day, Olive cleared away the teacups, saucers, and teaspoons, washed them right away and put them in her dish drainer. She hummed under breath as she moved to a comfy rocking chair to the side of the television. "I hope the TV will not disturb you. I want to watch Jeffersons."

"Hmm, no, that's okay. I'll just read the first two chapters and then go home. It's just that what you said, it floored me."

"Yeah, I felt the same way too when I learned this."

Olive did not respond but switched on the TV and was soon 'moving on up' with George and Louise Jefferson.

# PART 5: A QUICK IMPASSE

Kayla did not pretend when Simon walked through the door this time. She had not gone back to Olive for a couple days, because she was so busy processing her thoughts, and wanted to be alone to figure things out. She knew for a fact that nothing had changed with Simon and Emily. The woman was still in the picture, but the fact that their texts to each other were almost nonexistent puzzled Kayla and made her dig a little deeper. She tracked Simon's phone every day and realized that it would be stationary for about an hour and half at different times every day. He was meeting Emily; she was convinced. Immediately after that stationary period, platonic, work-related texts would resume on his personal phone. But there was no such communication before those meetings, they sprang up out of a clear blue heaven, so Kayla suspected he had another phone.

"Hi," Kayla chimed immediately Simon walked through the door.

"Hey," he replied.

She heard him take a deep breath; probably thought he was entering a war zone.

"How was your day?" he asked, testing the waters; it was so palpably different. It was incredibly hard admitting that she loved her cheating husband and still wanted him to love her and only her. Those desires left her vulnerable, at the mercy of his actions. The book had said to give a man unconditional respect, even when you didn't condone the hurt. That was her plan for the evening.

She could cuss that Eggerichs man who wrote that book. Did he interview any women about this point of view? Did any of them tell him how vulnerable he was asking us to be? To respect a man who cheated on you was turning yourself into nothing — where is that self-esteem? At least when you kicked and punched and bit him, you salvaged some pride, you masked the hurt, the fear, the inadequacy, and the rejection hiding inside you. And if you really went psycho on the side chick, sometimes they would chill, if only out of fear, knowing what you could do.

When however, you come at him with respect and love while he is still a cheat and a liar, it's like you are forced to sort through his hurt and selfishness to find the charred remains of your heart and hold it up to him for him to see.

"I need to talk to you 'cause I'm hurting," she raked out the words like blowing on hot coals. "So let me know when you can talk."

"Alright," Simon said. She could tell by his tone that he would listen to her, so she settled into her spot on the sofa, and switched on the TV to watch the news at 6. He poured himself a glass of wine, came to the living room and sat next to her. Kayla was surprised, something was changing before it happened, but she couldn't guess what. He seemed more responsive, but why? Nothing had changed except that the stupid book was changing her thoughts about Simon. Was it possible to feel someone's thoughts? Kayla shook the cobwebs out of her head; *focus on the news until he begins the conversation.*

"So what do you want to talk about?"

Kayla sat up, but didn't face Simon, she muted the tv and adjusted the blanket around her, staring into space. "Why are seeing someone else? I thought you loved me."

"I do."

"So why is there another woman in our marriage—again?" The pause between 'marriage' and 'again' reeked of acerbity, she did not cry but her voice told the pain she felt.

He sipped his wine. "I don't love anyone but you."

"But you're sleeping with another woman. Why?"

"Why?

"Yes, why?" Kayla's heart dropped... Simon did not deny his infidelity. My God, it was true, but she knew that already. Nevertheless, hearing him was as if a rusty nail was driven through her wounded heart all over again. Sometimes, when the truth falls in place just let yourself bleed out.

Simon sniffed; Kayla sensed he was uneasy. "I don't love her, but I got caught up. She needs me."

Kayla turned to face him. "I don't need you?"

"You're at your computer all day, making money. What do you need me for?"

"Foolish question! How can I show you I need you when you're busy all over the place cheating on me?"

Simon put down his glass. He was not angry, he walked with heavy steps to the bedroom, and didn't come out again for the night. Kayla stayed on the couch, staring at stationary lights around the condominium. After a very long pause, she did something she had not done in years, she prayed, "Lord, if you're out there, help me save my marriage".

# PART 6: TELL HIM HOW YOU HURT

The next day, Kayla showed up, uninvited, at Olive's door.

"Hi Miss Olive, do you have a few minutes?" It was exactly 10 am, so she knew the old lady would be settling down to watch another episode of the Jeffersons. She had already breakfasted and cleaned the house. Olive surveyed her closely. "I see you're reading the book. That's good."

Kayla nodded. She was halfway through Love & Respect and every chapter was making her feel more despondent. Her marriage felt hopeless, she did not know how to let go when Simon was still seeing someone else. His adultery was very disrespectful, yet the concept of unconditional respect meant that she had to give what she did not receive to a person who did not deserve it.

All the words came out in a mouthful on Olive's doorstep, as she opened her door a little wider to let Kayla in.

"So, what happened? How are the two of you making out?"

"He more or less admitted he is seeing Emily."

"Oh? Did you ask him why?"

"He said she needs him."

"What did you say to that?"

"I asked him what about me, whether I didn't need him too. But he told me that I'm at my computer all day making money, so how can I need him. I told him how could I show him I needed him when he was seeing someone else, and that was the end of our conversation."

By now, they were at the dining room table. Olive had her Bible open, and the Love & Respect book as well. What happened to her regular TV program? Kayla wondered.

"This is hard, Miss Olive. This is hard." Kayla cringed to avoid tears. "I cannot respect a man who is stepping out on me. It's revolting. Everything in me wants to hit out, cuss him, hurt him back like he is hurting me. The worst thing is I have no desire for anyone else but him."

"So do you want to hurt him, or do you want him to love you?" Olive asked, handing her a box of Kleenex.

"I can't make him love me, that is obvious. The guy is ruthless and selfish."

"Of course, they are selfish. Men are selfish by nature, very selfish. That is why in that same Ephesians Chapter 5 it says wives should respect their husbands; Paul also says to husbands to love their wives as they love their own selves. 'Cause God knew how selfish they are."

Kayla nodded, dabbing the corners of her eyes.

"So tonight, you begin by telling him what God says. He's only seeing things from his angle and not from yours. Time to bring God back into your marriage. Simon used to go to church too, didn't he?"

"Yes, we both did for a while. He gave his life to Christ too, a couple years after me."

"Okay, so y'all just rusty and he turn ratchet. I get it."

Kayla erupted into an uncontrollable fit of laughter. "Ratchet? Miss Olive what are you watching on TV?"

"Some Madea movie, I saw the other day. Y'all have

*confront sin, selfishness and uncaring behaviour*

terms for everything. We just used to say prostitute themselves in the past. But I hear that people don't say prostitute anymore." Miss Olive was all about business and wanted to talk. She didn't switch on the television while Kayla was with her.

"The respect part is only one segment in fixing a marriage. You must confront sin, selfishness, and uncaring behavior. Respect, however, is unconditional— you agree? And so is love. It's both, equally. Whether or not you disrespect your man, you are still a queen. You don't deserve to be sharing him; that's beneath your station as a wife."

"Then, what kind of king is that?"

"Eh eh. We agreed. What if you look at him as a king?"

"Well, that's one BAD king, Miss Olive. I'm not lying. I cannot see it."

"Well look, you said it yourself. Good king or bad king, but a king nonetheless. You don't ever treat a king like he's a pauper, whether he rules well or is doing a terrible job. You understand?"

Kayla nodded.

"But here's the thing. There's a way to get kings to be accountable, though. When Oscar was playing around, I fought with him, egged his car, stuffed ice cream up the muffler one time, even showed up at his workplace and made a stink. After I did all of that and it did not work, I began to treat him like a king."

"While he was still cheating on you?"

"Don't judge me before you hear the whole story. What I meant was that before, I used to call him the worst names in the book, nigga, yes, that was the 80s. Lowlife, Deadbeat, Trash. All the names. And because that's how I saw him, his actions matched who I thought he was. Next to our

*Think of him as a King and hold him to that standard* [handwritten note in top margin]

house was a neighbor, I'll never forget her. It was a white woman married to a Black man. When she heard what was happening in our home, she invited me to come sit with her. She was the one who taught me all the things I'm trying to teach you now. She was the one who introduced me to this book."

"I am still not sure how I should deal with Simon?"

"You need to show him that he is lowering himself by cheating on you. Think of him as a king and hold him to that standard. Tell him he is better and bigger than being a little adulterer. God said husbands are to love their wives as they love their own selves, and if he's not doing that, he will be judged accordingly. God does not play. Tell him that love is unconditional, whether you respect him or not, in the same way that respect is unconditional, whether he loves you or not. You must show him how his actions affect you and how much you hurt. The king in him will want to protect you."

"Then he will turn around next day and go back to that Emily woman. I can't risk that."

Olive responded so quickly that Kayla thought the old lady was about to box her as well. "Yes, you can," Olive blared out loud. "Yes, you can; risk it all! Your marriage is worth much more. That side woman is trash, rubbish, poo! Don't leave Simon for her."

"I'm so afraid to do all this and then see him walk all over me, sleeping with other women and expecting me to be waiting at home, cooking, loving and respecting him."

"What's the end result, Kayla. What-is-the-end-result?"

"I don't know. I truly don't know if I will ever have Simon's heart. I always remember that the only reason the last affair ended was because the woman left, not on account of my compelling powers as his wife."

49

"That was before you met me, before you read this book; before you decided to let God lead you in this fight. The Bible says here, in 2 Corinthians 10: 4 - 5." She passed the open Bible to Kayla and asked her to read the highlighted part.

'For the weapons of our warfare are not carnal but mighty in God for pulling down strongholds, casting down arguments and every high thing that exalts itself against the knowledge of God, bringing every thought into captivity to the obedience of Christ, and being ready to punish all disobedience when your obedience is fulfilled...'

"Yeah, I remember that verse."

"Most people focus on the spiritual weapons. Look at the last part about obedience. What is God saying there?"

"Being ready to punish all disobedience when your obedience is fulfilled?"

"Um, I don't know. "

"Yes you do. Take your time."

"Okay, the Paul guy is talking about what the weapons of spiritual warfare can accomplish, they have the power to destroy arguments, change your thoughts and also punish disobedience, but only when we obey. Isn't that it?"

Miss Olive stared at her. "Yes. Yes Kayla. Holy Spirit is giving clarity." Kayla awakened a bit. She dived back into the verses of Scripture as Miss Olive continued to guide her.

"Look at that last part. When you obey what God tells you, your prayers work to punish every transgression against you. What is God asking wives to do then? What is our obedience?"

"Respect bad kings, ha!" Kayla could not help the quip. The older lady shook her head.

"Cheeky girl!" They laughed and the mood lightened.

"So the spiritual weapons will take care of spiritual

*of Universal laws of*

problems - but it depends on our obedience. When you tell me that you can't make Simon leave the girl, you're right because at least you realize that there's an attraction that cannot be broken in the natural state. But you know what will make it break? Your obedience. That's it."

"I don't know, I don't know, Miss Olive."

"Kayla, when you say you don't know, you know what you sound like? It's like you came to God's store, and he tells you the price of that nice pair of shoes that you always wanted, and then you tell him, I don't know if that's the price! What's your problem? It's his store; he sets the terms and conditions. How can you doubt him when he is telling you what you have to do to get what you always wanted? See where I'm going?"

"Yes. God made marriage. He is telling me what I must do to save mine, and I'm here like Doubting Thomas."

"Exactly."

"I just keep remembering my mom. She was such a good wife. She stayed and she took it, and I really believe that is what killed her."

"What do you mean she "took it"?

"My father cheated on her so many times and she stayed."

"Staying does not mean acceptance. So many wives live in silent contempt and rebellion, they just live and wait for their husbands to die, without realizing that they are dying inside too. Don't mistake silence with acceptance, or silence with respect."

Kayla thought back to the times her mother ignored her father. They never touched, never kissed, never held hands, or even referred to each other by their names. It was always a nod here and frown there, tell your Father to do this, tell your father to do that. Yes, she knew it now, her mother never respected her father after he cheated on her...the love went cold.

"But some women, like you and I, will fight back openly. We will retaliate. It's just that you are fighting the battle wrong."

"I see that."

"Now you have the right weapons."

"I'll use them now that I have them, like you say."

"Well, you'll surely have your man back. That respect and love formula is an antibiotic, it was made for the disease called Emily! Fire for her! You will see!"

Miss Olive pretended to fire off a couple of gunshots in the air. Kayla laughed.

"Ay ay, Miss Olive! You're a gangster now? Did you learn that from a movie too?"

"No. I just felt like that when Oscar had his women on the side. It's the frustration, the pain of knowing your husband is too stupid to see that he is leaving something valuable in exchange for trash. I could have beaten up those women, if I did follow my mind, let me tell you. And him too. So you know that I know how you feel. You feel deceived. You were the one who was there with him when things were hard, when he was a nobody, and now she wants to come and lay claim. Any wife would feel angry."

She looked off in the distance as if she was back in a more turbulent time.

"I don't like to fight and not win, Miss Olive. That's why I don't try with love. I don't think I have the power to make a man love me. To me, that's all him."

"But who does have the power to turn a relationship around?"

"God, I guess."

"You guess? You're not sure?"

"No, I am now. God can turn it around."

"There's a verse I used to say repeatedly: '*The king's heart is in the hand of the Lord. Like the rivers of water, he turns it wherever he wishes.*' Proverbs 21 verse 1. You can use it if you want. Let God work on your king. It's God's Word, not yours, that will break that rock of adultery into pieces, watch and see."

"So what, say it over him while he is sleeping or something?"

"That won't work if you don't first believe in the Word of God. You have to start with belief. Spend a lot of time meditating on what God says about you, your marriage and about him. Say the scriptures over and over, several times a day. That's what I did. I used to be on the train and muttering that scripture under my breath. You have to meditate on it and put energy into believing and seeing yourself and your husband in love again.

"Hmmm," was all Kayla could muster. She was truly at the feet of her teacher.

"You have to claim your marriage before God. Marriage is when a man leaves his mother and father and becomes one with his wife. Not half, or quarter. The whole man belongs to you, his wife. That's your spiritual right. That's the covenant you and him made before God. You must fight with a sense that you are fighting for what is yours. God can return Simon's heart to you, You're his and he is yours in God's sight."

They were both quiet, contemplating the battle ahead.

# PART 7: THE STATE OF THE KINGDOM

To Kayla's surprise, there was takeout on the dinner table when she came home from doing grocery. It was Thursday, the usual day for her to go shopping at Superstore. Simon brought home Chinese food from Good Buddy, their favorite restaurant. "Oh wow, thank you," she said. Kayla was really hungry, and sat down to eat, having washed her hands, not bothering to put the grocery away first. Miss Olive's sarcastic comment about how she would have felt if she prepared the food and Simon said he was not hungry, came to mind. Gosh she had been a fool. The Crispy Ginger chicken was always so good, as was the egg fried rice. "What did you order for yourself?" she asked Simon, curious as to what was on his plate. He usually went with the Ginger Beef but seemed to have ordered something different today.

"Oh, that's duck,"

"Duck?" Kayla chuckled. "Since when you eating duck?"

"Well when I went to order, the lady suggested I try it. Here, do you want to taste?"

And her cheating Simon cut a piece of his BBQ duck, and holding her gaze with a ruthless boldness that made her insides flip, asked her to open her mouth and laid it gently on her tongue. The gesture, and his eyes while he did it, sweeping up to meet hers, were exciting. Kayla heard herself say 'yuck" when she realized that she didn't fancy the blandness in her mouth. Next, she was spitting out the morsel on her side plate, bursting into tears. Simon put the fork down. "Hey, hey, I didn't mean to force you to eat it." But Kayla could not stop crying. This was more than a mere Thursday night dinner. Why was he reminding her of the man he could be? Why be nice and caring and irresistible and still be cheating? Did he not realize how much she wanted him, that she would forever want him, be moved by him, be stirred by him? Simon moved over and held her; she sobbed on his shoulder. He lifted her like she weighed ten pounds and carried her to the sofa. They sat together, her head nestled under his neck, for a couple minutes. The steady rise and fall of his chest calmed Kayla. "There's a book I think we should both read," she said when her throat was clear.

"Okay."

She got up, retrieved her copy of 'Love and Respect' from her handbag on the kitchen counter and handed it to him. He flipped through and asked, "Where did you get this? Who's Olive?" He read the dedication Olive wrote on the inside page next to the Table of Contents.

"The lady next door."

"The nosey lady everyone is complaining about. The same one we caught peeping through the blinds when I came home with the new car?"

"Yes, her," Kayla smiled. She had forgotten how they had laughed at the surreptitious twitching of the blinds in Olive's bedroom that looked down over their parking stall.

"She heard us fighting the other night. Came over to talk to me the next day."

They said nothing for about a minute. Kayla could tell

that Simon felt embarrassed. Suddenly, he changed the subject.

"What is the guy saying anyway?" He raised the book before dropping it on the center table next to them.
"Men don't need love and women don't need respect?"
He scoffed a little, but Kayla ignored him. She too had felt the same way at first.
"He's actually saying that although both men and women need love and respect, men's highest need is respect and a woman's highest need is love."

"Oh," Simon said, as if he had just discovered a hidden sore.

More silence, but he picked up the book and thumbed through it again. Kayla tried to appear nonchalant, but shifted her eyes, straining to see what he was looking for. How on earth did Simon head straight for Chapter 15, she would never know. It was the chapter titled "How to Spell Respect to Your Husband". He looked all smug and pleased as he traced the words with his finger, pointing and tapping repeatedly. Kayla shook her head in amazement. "Why did you skip the first chapter? Did you see it? It's called *"How to Spell Love to Your Wife!"* All she could hear was Olive's voice in her head. *"Men are selfish. That's why God told them to love their wives as they love themselves."*
Simon winced, as if expecting Kayla to attempt to hit him. The smugness lifted like a fog off his face.
"I am not sharing you with anyone else again, Simon. I don't deserve that," she sat back without looking at him, but feeling him squirm.
"The thing is, I'm your wife. God is going to judge you on how you treat me. I know we've stopped going to church and praying together, but that does not mean He's given up on us. "

"Yeah, we have to start doing that again," Simon stared wildly at nothing.

"Before God, we still signed up to be each other's forever. Miss Olive was showing me the part in the Bible that says if a husband deals treacherously with the wife of his youth, God will punish him."

"Okay." He paused.

"You don't really need me from what I see."

"That's not a reason to step out on me."

"You don't call me at work. You don't notice me. You don't even know what I do, nor do you care." Simon shrugged. He was about to go on but decided against it.

"Simon, you're hurting me more than you think."

"So what about me? Don't you think I'd love to come home knowing you made some time for me."

"I'd like if you stopped seeing that stupid woman for a start."

"You told me you deserve love and loyalty no matter what. I deserve your attention and respect..."

The minute Simon said respect, he looked exposed as if someone wrenched his protective shield away from him. He got up and went to pour himself a glass of wine.

"Do you want a drink?" he motioned to Kayla.

"No, I'm fine, thanks," she did not recognize her small, fine voice. She felt invisibly small having just heard her man tell her that she made him feel invisible. "So does she make you feel better than I do?"

"I'll take care of that, Kayla."

"That's not what I asked you, Simon! What does she do that I don't?" She started working herself into shouting mode, as always, and then suddenly lowered her voice. *That's not how you fight like a wife.*

He stood with his back to her and she could see his

chest heaving. Simon's broad shoulders were taut, his back strong, like he could carry the world if asked. Her eyes naturally lowered to take in his tight butt, looking tighter as he seemed to clench the cheeks together. "Tell me, what does she give you that I don't?"

Simon scoffed. He looked like he was about to answer her, but caught himself just in time.

"Listen, you are my wife, no one else. I messed up. I'll take care of it, I tell you."

He said nothing more. She ended up drinking a glass of wine after all, but did not follow him into the bedroom, despite the urge driving her mad.

# PART 8: AN ENCOUNTER LIKE NO OTHER

Kayla woke up about 3 am with echoes of shouts in her head. Was she dreaming? She could have been, for he stood with his back to her... with his back to her... with his back to her... She swore that she heard someone shout at her to get up. She jumped off the bed in the spare room and rushed to the master bedroom. The door was unlocked, the curtains drawn. From the lamplight streaming into her bedroom, she could see that Simon was in a deep sleep, lying on his back, mouth open, chest bare, possibly stark naked save for the sheet around his midsection. She quietly closed the door despite the instant rush of excitement she felt savoring him, innocent and helpless on the bed. Lord, if it was not for the urgency of that voice in her heart, she would forget all the wrong he had done and slide into that bed with him.

But now was not the time.

There was that voice, an urgent murmur in her head as she made her way in the dark towards the living room.

"I love you."

She knew that voice, had heard it through her teen years, had trusted it until the trust wore thin. But here they were.

"I never left you. I love you. I love Simon. Ask me."

"Ask you what?"

Before she knew it, she was sure that God was speaking to her again. These thoughts were not hers, and too besides, she remembered that voice, all too familiar and loving, that had been with her up until Simon had stepped out on her that first time. Afterwards she severed all ties with the divine. Because as far as she was concerned, if God were powerful, there was no way he would have let her feel so abandoned as a wife.

But she could not help wanting to hear this voice now. It was like a quiet fire burning in her, longing for her to connect again. Kayla sat in her favorite spot on the sofa, close to the large bay window that looked out on their small backyard.

"Alright God. What?"

"I love you."

"Yeah, I know." Why was she hearing these words with such urgency? She may have doubted her faith, but she always knew God loved her.

"Do you believe in me?"

"Yes, I do." She was literally having a conversation with that voice. She wasn't even trying to doubt it.

"Do you trust me?" No she didn't.

"No."

"Trust me."

"You left me the first time."

"You left me the first time. I was always here."

Kayla's knees buckled under her. It was true.

"I don't know how to trust you again."

"Hebrews 11:1"

"What about it?"

"Read it."

Kayla sighed. It was like old times. That soft, pleasing voice in her head, like the murmuring of a brook. She went to the bookshelf for her Bible; it had been sitting there for MONTHS, wedged between The Intelligent Investor and Rich Dad, Poor Dad. She flipped to Hebrews 11, verse 1 and whispered aloud as if she had never strayed from God.
'Now faith is the assurance (title deed, confirmation) of things hoped for, (divinely guaranteed) ...Title deed. Title deed. Title deed. Title deed? Somehow these words kept jumping off the paper. She read till the end of the verse, "and the evidence of things not seen." Somehow, her eyes stuck onto the words 'title deed.' It seemed like a key to something.

Kayla drew her blanket around her tightly, her mind questioning.
*But how God? I've already lost him.*
"No you haven't. He's yours. You're his. You have the rights."

Suddenly, she was outside of herself, like in a movie, holding a burning parchment in her hand. Somehow she knew what it was, her marriage certificate; it felt heavy. And there was Anna; she came from nowhere and reached out to grab the marriage certificate. Kayla froze, fear filling her heart. Anna observed and laughed, becoming bolder, her eyes were on Simon who had magically appeared by Kayla's side. Anna stepped forward, her breasts exposed, and heaving sensuously, crying for Simon while she snatched the title deed from Kayla. Kayla let her marriage certificate slip from her grasp as Simon showed much more than an inclination to move over to Anna. Kayla's fears intensified beyond fever pitch. *Simon no longer loved her. Anna was more attractive. He doesn't love me anymore. I don't care, I'm not fighting for man, I'm going to let him go.* As she watched, Anna twisted the marriage certificate into a wedding ring that she slipped on her middle finger, and smiled bewitchingly at Simon.

What was this? A vision? A trance? Kayla shook herself in a vain struggle to return to reality. She had let someone take what was hers because she didn't think it belonged to her alone. You cannot fake the feeling of being robbed; it's a singular feeling, worse than empty. Only the victim knows. You feel like zero. Kayla, now experiencing a bout of weightlessness, dropped to her knees.

"Lord, I come to claim what is mine, in Jesus' name. I claim my husband. I claim him before you. He is mine. Thank you, I take back the title deed that is made in our name, not hers. She is the zero, not me. I take back the title deed, Amen."

Now she believed Olive; now she knew why she could fight like a wife, because she was fighting for what was hers anyways.

Before she could say another word of triumph, Kayla heard a big, challenging question. *"What do wives do?"* The quiet brook bubbled in her head, insistent.

She dreaded the answer, sucked her teeth, shook her head. The voice within her did not ask again but gave instructions.

"You're a wife. Do what wives do."

Why would she go to bed with him now? Why? She knew instinctively that was what she was being asked to do, to let him in again. She saw herself like a reflection in a room size mirror, straddling Simon, her body laying claim, expropriating parameters, while he with little effort probed into some of her deepest recesses, places she had closed off, but was permitting him to enter without as much as a half-hearted no. She felt the rhythm of her quiet determination, steady though quite vulnerable. She felt a softening of spirit, he wanted to lodge in that space all along, but after the betrayal, she would not let him, although she always believed that he was hers. There was a renewed confidence bubbling in her veins. She would make him explode with ecstasy when she became brave enough to show herself to him again.

"Go back to your bed."

Kayla knew what she had to do. She approached the bedroom, opened the door. Simon, if he had been sleeping, was no longer. She knew, because he caught his breath and exhaled way too carefully, he was waiting to see what she would do. No way, no way would she give herself to him anymore. Kayla turned around in disgust and hurried to the spare room.

# PART 9: THE EAGLET GROWS HER WINGS

As soon as Simon left for work in the morning, Kayla got on her knees again. "Lord, help me. Help me. I want my husband back."

She was like a zealot, fanatical, but without the fire and brimstone in her eyes. Kayla cried so much her nose got stuffy, but she kept on praying. *Title deed. Her man belonged to her.*

"Lord, you told me my husband is mine. Return him to me. Return him to me. Return Simon to me please," she sobbed and hiccupped.

The voice came sometime in the morning. "Take what is yours. Fight because he is yours, that's faith."

When Kayla showed up at Olive's door, later that day, she looked like a warrior who had lost this battle but found the weapons she needed to win the war. It was a rest stop, a solemn one. She would have to humble herself, fight the bitterness, and trust God with her marriage.

"God spoke to me this morning, Miss Olive. But I checked Simon's texts this morning, and she is still texting him and he is responding, calling her baby and promising to meet her after work."

"I thought you said they were using another phone?"

"I thought so. Maybe he does not care to hide it anymore. I saw those texts today, while he was in the shower."

"Okay, call him, tell him that you need him after work. Tell him you want him to come home."

"I can't do that. He'll choose to stay with her and that will break me in bits."

Olive stared at Kayla, it was one of those moments when her eyes seemed to slip past her into the great beyond, it gave Kayla the chills. This was not the first time.

"Go back home, Kayla. Bring everything eating out your craw to God. Remember you have the title deed. It's valid."

*There, that phrase again.*

"Call your husband and let him know you need him tonight. Stop being good, stop doing what Simon expects. Start being a wife."

Olive's soul-piercing eyes burned into Kayla's face. It felt like the old lady was summoning her to war. "And let me know tomorrow how it went."

Kayla spun on her heel. She got to her house on autopilot and marched straight to the spare room. Where was her marriage certificate? At least she could duplicate that part of her vision. She was going to God with it. She found it in its special box. She prayed over it, calling Simon's name over and over again. In the name of Jesus, he is mine. Lord, I bring the title deed of my marriage to you. Thank you for my husband and for this title deed, the substance of my hope, the evidence of my faith in the marriage which you have blessed. All I ask of you is to turn his heart back to me again. Turn his heart to me again. Turn his heart to me again. The king's heart is in your hands. Simon's heart is in your hands, Lord. Like the rivers of water, thank you Lord, that my husband chooses me over all others. Thank you, Lord, for my title deed that is not in vain."

In her mind's eye, she saw all the proud women lining up to laugh at her, scoff at her, call her desperate. She saw their raised eyebrows, their knowing smiles, their haughty noses. They scorned her for believing in love. They were literally laughing at her. But she did not care.

She kept on pleading.

Kayla cannot explain even to the most extremely religious sect what happens to her next. She breaks out speaking in ancient tongues and is helpless as the room transforms into palatial quarters fit for a king and his queen. In her mind's eye she sees a military figure, suited in burnished armor, more dazzling than the sun, so bright she cannot see his face, only he is dressed for battle. In that split second, Kayla understands that heaven is on the side of the scorned wife, the cheated, the abused, and the ridiculed wife. She also understands that she must fight to regain what's hers. The voice that speaks to her from the inner chambers of her heart is insistent and determined.

Kayla falls on her face and prays. She cusses, cries, pleads with God and then rejoices as visions of Simon and herself dart across the movie screen housed in her theatre of thoughts. They are holding hands walking along a sandy shore; then they are in a steamy bedroom setting, smothered among the sheets; now he is smiling at her again, embracing her. His phone rings, he switches it off. It rings again. He cuts off the call. She watches him do it as plain as day right in front of her. Kayla falls asleep on the floor, praying.

When she woke up, she speed dialed Simon.

"Hey," he said. "What's up?" He was businesslike, she knew what was going on. Emily was probably nearby. The good, old girl Kayla would have folded back into her shell and shouted never mind into the phone. Maybe the old Kayla would not have called at all, because she knew the hidden memo Simon passed on to her again and again, "Don't bother me."

Today, she chose to reject that memo.

Kayla sat up with her title deed in hand as she spoke to him. "Hey baby, how are you? Can you come home? I promise no arguments, no fights, no negatives. I need you."

She bit her lip hoping he was not going to be rude and say that he was working, only for her to check the texts and see that he was in bed with his other woman.

"Oh," was all Simon said for the first 10 or 15 seconds. Then she heard him draw a long breath and sigh: "Okay, I'll come. See you soon."

He was going to come home at her request, Kayla was shocked. What in God's name was happening? She put down the phone, bemused.

Kayla spent the rest of the day on a high. Till now, she believed God had let her down. However, the last few days, she felt the presence of divinity. She found herself thanking God for her husband, seeing, and loving him, his body, his habits, his presence. Minute by minute she was being changed by her prayers.

And yet there was a part of her where doubt lingered. Was her mind playing tricks on her, or was this a display of God's power? Trust the devil to meddle with details.

She had to try though. Simon was choosing her over his outside woman; he was coming home to be with her! Kayla cooked his favorite dish, Chicken Piccata Pasta, something she had not done in years. It was a delicious dish, tangy, savory, and heady with dry white wine. She had been meaning to cook this for some time, but Simon's shenanigans made her lose all interest.

# PART 10: GIRL, BYE

By four, the table was set for dinner, Kayla put everything out: the dinnerware, the special Waterford crystal goblets that her godmother gifted them as a wedding present, the special cloth napkins that she bought at Crate and Barrel at Southgate Mall their first Christmas in Edmonton, and her finest silverware. There was a part of her that nagged still. *Simon was still sleeping with Emily, he was still texting her, planning dates and downplaying his relationship with his wife. Why on earth was Kayla going out of her way for him like that.*

"Because your thoughts have changed," a voice whispered back to her.

Never had there been such a time that she felt so at ease to serve her husband. This grace did not come to her from within, she knew that, not when she thought of Simon and what he had done.

She drew a bath, and sat in a cloud of vanilla and peony bath bombs, soaked in her imagination, immersed in what she would do when he came home.

When the key turned in the lock, Kayla experienced a feeling of contentment, already she had outdone herself .

"Hey," she said, as he entered, his eyes narrowed to slits, watching her with suspicion. He relaxed on seeing her smile.

"Thanks for coming home straight. I just wanted you here. It gets lonely working from home, for real."

"I thought you liked being by yourself, making your own money and all that," he grinned.

Kayla saw a sliver of doubt in his eyes, and it dawned on her that Simon did not know she appreciated his work.

"Hey, you know we need your money too. Ever since you got this job it's been easier on us. Thank you."

Simon's face softened, his shoulders relaxed a little, he rubbed the back of his neck, something he did when he was thinking, then sniffed and made a beeline for the kitchen; midway he stopped, confused.

"I thought you cooked?" he said, turning to her in the living room.

"I did," She said, with the confidence of Mrs. Kayla Johnson. "Dinner is on the table."

For a moment, he said nothing but walked to the dining table and stood dumbfounded. "Hope you don't have an imaginary client on the phone?" he quipped.

Kayla glared at him and then burst out laughing. "How did you know I was faking?"

"When?"

"The other day".

"You were talking about something on the screen that wasn't there. I saw when I passed around you."

"Well, you do the same thing, pretend to be sleeping when you're not," Kayla shot back. She was supposed to be in control, but Simon was calling her out.

"Old trick. We both do it, and we know. Maybe I'm waiting for you to come on to me." Simon looked vulnerable; Kayla wanted to spare him and turned away.

*Come on to him? He'll think he's a cheese or something. No sir, I will keep my dignity.*

The pasta was tender, and the combination of capers, garlic and white wine was surreal, the taste of the moment. While they were eating, Simon's phone vibrated. He winced. Kayla pretended not to notice; she also saw something else; he took a sneak peek at the incoming message. Her heart sank, but her mind was alive with drumbeats— title deed... title deed. The title deed that told heaven's army, her husband was hers. *Help me, Lord. Let him choose me. Let him.*

The phone stopped blinking, they talked and laughed like they were just married, but Kayla was wary. Simon was deceitful, he had been texting Emily just before he got home. Their conversation was burned into Kayla's memory.

*"Hey, have to go home, but I'll call you later."*

*"Wife acting up?"*

*"No, just some stuff we must do. Can't be avoided."*

*"I love you."*

*"Yeah."*

*"I said I love you."*

*"I said yeah, you do. You know what you mean to me. I'll call you later."*

She wanted to bring it up and took a sip of wine. Title deed, she was the wife, the boss, not Emily. *'And to be fair,'* a rational voice whispered, *'he has never told Emily that he loved her. Not once.'* In all the time she had been monitoring his phone, Simon had never uttered those words.

Kayla went deep into herself to retrieve her wounded pride to bring before her Father and lay it all out for him. She didn't want anyone else to see. Her heart was bursting with shame and embarrassment, but she laid it down before God.

Simon cleared away the dishes and Kayla packed up the

dishwasher, just like old times. They were easy with each other, and Kayla relaxed a little, enough to flirt with him. She stared at him with intention as he handed her a plate over the dishwasher. He smiled back. Passed so close to her that it was not a mistake. The air was thick with awkward expectations. Afterwards, she excused herself while Simon was watching the news and went into the bedroom. If she was going to do this, better do it while she held her nerve.

He glimpsed Kayla passing through the hallway to the kitchen, a swish of her short, red lace baby doll catching his eye as she opened the fridge. Before she knew it, Simon reached the kitchen; up hard behind her, kissing her neck, hands all over caressing her body. They did not make it to the bedroom, the kitchen counter served the same desperate purpose as would the bed if they held out. He was again like a wild stud in her field, thrusting and burrowing through every cavern he found. Afterwards he buried his head in her neck and moaned. She held him until the tenseness in his body eased, neither of them sure whether the world was still turning, or that Good Friday still fell on a Friday. Who was the conqueror and who was the conquered, remained the unanswered question.

His phone was nearby during all this, it vibrated again, though the screen stayed dark. He swore under his breath and cut it off. It rang again, almost sounding angry this time. Simon cut off the incoming call. Kayla was angry. Enough now. That Emily had to go. She disentangled from Simon, tracing a finger down his chest. "That was the first round. Let's have dessert in the bedroom, but go shower first. I don't want to taste me in my mouth."

"*Lord, please make him leave his phone behind,*" she prayed, and strangely, he did. He left it on the counter, went to the bedroom, stripped and strode into the shower like a peacock. Kayla brought the phone to the room, and just before she climbed into bed, she quickly unlocked his phone and pressed redial. She had memorized his passcode, and never let him even suspect that she knew it. She lowered the volume to zero, and hid the phone on the top shelf of the walk-in closet, near the bed.

She was noisy and slurpy and remembered how he was when she went down on him. He'd moan and chant her name. There's much more to be done if you knew the side chick is listening. Simon was loud in bed and did not hold back. He placed his hand on Kayla's head, regulating her rhythm, while she did the magic with the twirl of her tongue and her cheeks. Simon moaned and shouted his hallelujah chorus like a freshly converted Soca Baptist, repeating her name, swearing he missed her, and he was sorry. She grasped his manhood between her thumb and index finger and in between breaths, told him how much of a man he was. She told him no one could take his place, that every part of her belonged to him and she was hungry for his love. He told her all the things he wanted to do to her, called her his woman, his bitch; said dirty things to her until her whole body screamed for more of him inside her. Kayla swiveled, her mouth clamped around his member, eager to see if the call had ended. It had not. Emily was still on the phone, listening. Simon climaxed in full masculine glory; the lion aroused beyond expectations by his lioness. Kayla swallowed every bit of him.

"You did that? What's going on with you? Why you so djanmèt?"

"A new trick I decided to try. It's reserved for kings only." Kayla grinned.

"Oh, so what? I'm a king?" Simon looked so pleased with

himself that Kayla wanted to revert to her old, cynical thoughts. Men were just so self-centered.

"Yup. You're my king. This is the royal treatment."

"Well, if I'm a king, you're a queen. You deserve a royal service. Come to papa, let him fix you."

He pulled her to him, flipped her over on her back — other horizons, other dawns awakened. Another round later, they both lay spent across the bed, naked like Adam and Eve on that first morning when she gorged on the forbidden fruit.

Simon looked her over on their bed, his eyes devouring her plump figure. He looked like a king surveying his conquered kingdom.

"This never happened so quick?" He grinned.

She delivered a kallòt to the side of his head. "So you making fun of me?"

"Well for all your talk...scratching my car, cussing me out and even biting me ... I guess I can still make you lose it ..."

"Well for all your stepping out on me.... you're still mine."

She was raw and in awe when she said it, and he felt how much it meant to her.

He propped himself up on his elbows, staring down at her with knowing.

"I don't belong to anyone but you Kayla. I love you. You're my wife." The way he looked at her made her heart weak. They cuddled in the unbelievable afterglow of their lovemaking, Kayla noting that Simon did not for once look around for his phone; he was totally into Kayla, with eyes for no other. He wrapped his arms around her, fondling her breasts.

"Your arms are too heavy, woy!"

"Really? I was not too heavy a while ago?"

She elbowed him, embarrassed and happy at the same time.

He told her of his plans and how he wanted to move on from this job, insisting that it was temporary, and maybe he should start sending out applications. Kayla knew what he really meant to say. That he would leave this job so that he didn't have to deal with the romantic entanglement anymore. Again, Kayla assured him that she was happy he loved to work and provide for them. They chatted until Simon fell asleep.

Kayla waited, once she was sure that Simon's breathing became regular, she eased out of his embrace and went for the phone. She held it to her ear. Emily was weeping uncontrollably at the other end. *Byen fèt.* The words that were on the tip of Kayla's tongue to say were not pleasant, maybe she should go outside. But she looked back at her sleeping husband and knew that her revenge was not revenge, but a complete victory. Words were nothing. The real triumph was in whether Emily still had Kayla's husband. Judging by everything that had just happened, SHE DID NOT.

Kayla ended the call. Girl bye.

# ABOUT THE AUTHOR

## Lisa M. Dublin

Lisa Dublin was born in Saint Lucia and moved to Canada with her husband and three sons in 2013. She is a writer, speaker, performance poet and certified life coach.

She writes from a deep place of honesty and understanding of human nature and from all her experiences as an entrepreneur, mom, wife, CEO of her own personal development company, television and radio presenter, producer and now citizen of a new country.

The recipient of a Silver M&C Fine Arts Award for Short Fiction in 2003, she has also earned acclaim as a powerful performance poet, having won two national competitions in Saint Lucia in the early 2000s.

# BOOKS BY THIS AUTHOR

## How George Jones Saved Christmas

Twelve-year-old Christy loves everything about Christmas in Saint Lucia: awakening to the smell of delicious beef and pork stewing on coal pots, playing dolls with her cousin Sweetie, and of course, singing along to the music of George Jones.

The traditions are threatened when a quarrel breaks out between Christy's mother, Merm, and her aunt Mabel. It's not just a minor tiff between sisters, either: they are so angry with each other that Mabel threatens to spend Christmas with her family in a hotel, and Merm declares that her own family — Christy and her siblings — will spend Christmas Day by themselves.

Heartbroken at the thought of spending the holiday apart, Christy and Sweetie hatch a plan to make the adults in their lives reconsider what Christmas is truly all about. What they discover about the bonds of family—and the powerful sentimentality of country music—will resonate with anyone who has ever felt frustrated by the people they love most.

Tender and nostalgic, How George Jones Saved Christmas

is a story of complex family dynamics as seen through the eyes of a precocious young girl.

## Sani Baat: A Voice Throwing

This is Lisa's first chapbook collection of poetry. It is only available from the author herself. Interested in buying a copy? Send her an email: lisa@lisamdublin.com

# WATCH OUT FOR THE NEXT BOOK IN THE 'KINDLE A BURNING' SERIES!

Kindle a
burning

# CONNECT WITH ME!

## I'd love to connect with you!

### Please follow my Author page on Amazon:
https://www.amazon.com/stores/Lisa-Dublin/author/
B0762R5FCT?
ref=ap_rdr&store_ref=ap_rdr&isDramIntegrated=true&sh
oppingPortalEnabled=true

### You can also write a great review of my book here:

https://www.amazon.com/Good-Girl-Gone-Wife-
Burning-ebook/dp/B0CMMRYKGG?ref_=ast_author_mpb

### And here's how we can connect!

Email: lisa@lisamdublin.com
Website: www.lisamdublin.com
Facebook: @lisamdublin
IG: https://www.instagram.com/lisamdublin/
Linkedin: https://www.linkedin.com/in/lisadublin/

Manufactured by Amazon.ca
Bolton, ON

36401447R00049